# If you can...

# We can...

Beth Shoshan & Petra Brown

Albury Books

I love you…

      … I really do!

(Although my arms are just too small
and so I can't quite cuddle you)

I hug you…

… you hug me

(And round
and round
we dance together,
holding tight.

Don't let me fall!)

I tickle you...

    ... you giggle too

(But not my toes...! No!
Not my toes,
you know that's when I'll squeal the most!)

I make you laugh ...
... you laugh with me

(There's nothing in this world
can make us feel so good
as laughter can, as laughter does,
as laughter should)

I hold your hand...
... you hold mine tight

(Just feeling snug, secure and safe.
Just knowing you'll protect me,
care for me...
... be there)

I sing you songs…
… you sing them too

(Loud ones, soft ones,
make me laugh ones.
Love songs, sleep songs,
safe and sound songs)

I tell you tales…
… you listen close

(Then tell me stories
through the night…

Of mighty dragons,
gallant knights…

adventures made
to fill my mind)

I'm in your dreams...
... and you're
in mine.

(The best dreams, safe dreams,
sleep all night dreams.
My dreams, your dreams.
Always our dreams)

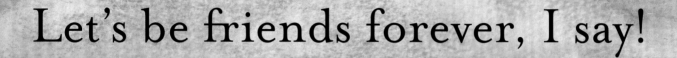

Let's be friends forever, I say!

There for one another,
looking out and taking care.

So…

Whatever you do…

and whatever I do...

Let's do it...